American edition published in 2014 by Andersen Press USA,
an imprint of Andersen Press Ltd.
www.andersenpressusa.com
First published in Great Britain in 2014 by Andersen Press Ltd.,
20 Vauxhall Bridge Road, London SW1V 2SA.
Distributed in the United States and Canada by Lerner Publishing Group, Inc.
241 First Avenue NorthMinneapolis, MN 55401 USA
For reading levels and more information, look up this title at www.lernerbooks.com.
Printed and bound in Malaysia by Tien Wah Press.
Library of Congress Cataloging-in-Publication data available.
ISBN: 978-1-4677-6315-8 eBook ISBN: 978-1-4677-6319-6
1 – TWP – 4/15/14

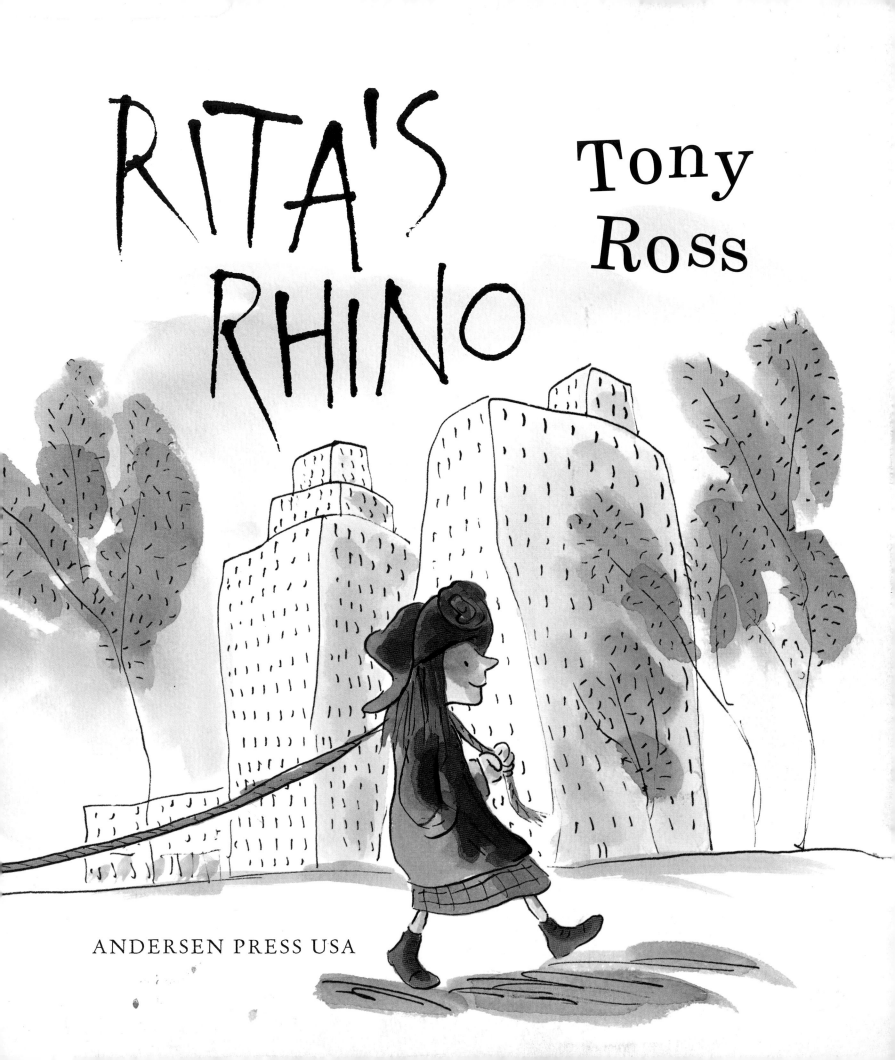

RITA'S RHINO

Tony Ross

ANDERSEN PRESS USA

When Rita asked for a pet, her mom said, "NOOOOOOO! Pets are stinky, greedy things. You have to clean up after them and take them for walks."
"I'll do that," said Rita. "PLEASE!"
"All right," said Mom, "you can have a very little pet."

A few days later, Mom gave Rita a jar.
"Meet your new pet flea, Harold," she said.
"Poo, I can't even see him!" Rita snorted.

"Frogs make wonderful pets," said Uncle Eric, handing Rita a tadpole.
"Sometimes, if you kiss them, they turn into princes."
"I don't want a prince," frowned Rita. "I want a pet!"

Rita decided to find a pet for herself, so she set off to the zoo.
As she reached the rhinoceros cage, it began to rain.
"I hate the rain," groaned the rhinoceros.

"Would you like to come home with me?" asked Rita. "It's dry there."
"Yes, please," said the rhinoceros, squeezing through the bars of his cage.

Rita put her hat and coat over the rhinoceros,
so the zookeeper would not notice . . .

and the two of them walked out of the zoo.

When they reached the block where Rita lived, it was a bit
of a squeeze, getting her new pet into the elevator.

It was not easy hiding a rhinoceros in a small bedroom in a small apartment.
Mom brought Rita toast covered with marmalade.
As soon as she left, Rita gave it to her pet.
"I don't like toast," said the rhinoceros. "I only eat grass from Africa."
"Goodness," said Rita. "You'd better come with me."

"I only have half a bag of grass from Africa
left and it's very expensive," said the pet-shop man.
Rita frowned and emptied her purse. She looked at the rhinoceros,
"When that's gone, it'll have to be marmalade toast for you."

GRASS From Africa

Pet Cows for SALE

Almost clean Apply ____

LOST

LOST. Pet worm answers to Philip

HOME WANTED FOR TYSON

Sometimes, Rita began to wish she did not have a pet rhinoceros. She loved him, of course, but it would have been so much better if he were not so large. It was unpleasant hiding the piles of rhinoceros poop every day.

Sometimes, the rhinoceros missed the zoo, his comfy bed, his grass from Africa, and he always hated going up and down in the elevator.

When Rita went back to school, she took her rhinoceros with her. She left him outside with his horn stuck firmly in the ground to stop him rolling over. Rita wagged her finger at him. "Stay!" she said sternly.

"Is that a rhinoceros?" asked her teacher,
who was a bit near-sighted.
"No," said Rita. "That's my bouncy castle."

"A BOUNCY CASTLE!" whooped the
other children, rushing outside to play.

Much as he loved Rita, the rhinoceros decided enough was enough.

That night, he crept
away, back to the zoo.

The rhinoceros was happy to be back. But as he lay on his comfy bed
and nibbled his grass from Africa, he often thought of Rita,
and when he did, he shed a little tear.

And when Rita remembered her rhinoceros, she shed a little tear too.

But every summer after that, Rita took the rhinoceros to the beach for a few days, and they always had such a great time together that the rhinoceros was quite content to eat seaweed for a change.